zenda

The Impossible Butterfly

Dedicated to:

Birdie & Margie
Johnny & Gena, John, Mena, James & Anna

Special Thanks to:

Pam Amodeo
Bunny
Broadthink
The Two Camilles
Janine Drozd
Mary Ann Wheaton
Caspar, Lupe & Charlotte at Amodeo Petti

zenda

The Impossible Butterfly

created by
Ken Petti and John Amodeo

written with
Cassandra Westwood

Grosset & Dunlap • New York

Copyright © 2004 by Ken Petti & John Amodeo. ZENDA is a trademark of Ken Petti & John Amodeo. All rights reserved. Published by Grosset & Dunlap, a division of Penguin Young Readers Group, 345 Hudson Street, New York, New York 10014. GROSSET & DUNLAP is a trademark of Penguin Group (USA) Inc. Printed in the U.S.A.

Library of Congress Cataloging-in-Publication Data

Petti, Ken.
The impossible butterfly / created by Ken Petti and John Amodeo ; written with Cassandra Westwood.
p. cm. — (Zenda ; 5)
Summary: Zenda's return to school in the fall brings interesting challenges—a new girl who seems to be stealing all of Zenda's friends, and a caterpillar that she must care for until it turns into a butterfly.
ISBN 0-448-43257-9 (pbk.)
[1. Fantasy.] I. Amodeo, John, 1949 May 19- II. Westwood, Cassandra. III. Title.
PZ7.P448125Im 2004
[Fic]—dc22

2004007093

ISBN 0-448-43257-9   10 9 8 7 6 5 4 3 2 1

Contents

Sometimes I think being twelve-and-a-half is the hardest thing ever!

On my planet, Azureblue, it's supposed to be a very special time. Every girl or boy gets a special crystal ball called a gazing ball. You study it for six months, and it reveals musings that will help you on life's path.

Gazing ball study isn't hard, but because of my impatience, I had to see my gazing ball early and I broke it by mistake. The ball shattered into pieces! The missing pieces come to me as I live my life and learn new things. When I find all of the pieces and learn all of the musings, my ball will be complete.

It hasn't been easy. In fact, everything's

been crazy since I broke my gazing ball. I've been accidentally transported to another dimension and I got lost on a moon. And Alexandra White, a girl from my school, has been making my life absolutely miserable.

I used to think Alexandra was my biggest problem at school. But after we all got back from a school trip, I found out that there were other challenges waiting for me at school. Big ones.

These might just be my biggest challenges yet. I hope I figure out how to deal with them so I can earn more musings!

Cosmically yours,
Zenda

Willow

"Zenda! It's getting late!"

The sound of her mother's voice caused Zenda to look up from her journal. Zenda was in the round cupola off her bedroom, sitting cross-legged on a turquoise silk pillow. Her dog, Oscar, sat at her feet, staring up at her with his brown eyes. The morning sun streamed through the windows, casting a pale yellow glow over everything: more colorful pillows, uneven stacks of books, and Zenda's long, reddish-gold hair.

"I'll be right down!" Zenda called. She wanted to finish her journal entry.

⸻

It's been two days since we got back from our survival trip to Aquaria. Verbena and Vetiver have been so nice! Vetiver made wild mushroom crepes last night for dinner, and he even gathered the

2

mushrooms himself. And Verbena gave me a day off from harvesting the spikeberry patch. I know they were both worried about me when Mykal, Camille, Alexandra, and I got lost on Aquaria. But I know they're proud, too, because we safely found our way back to camp.

I'm pretty proud of myself too. I did a lot of things I never thought I'd be able to do, like camp out overnight, face my fears, and stand up to Alexandra.

I'm sure Alexandra will have something to say about that at school today, but I'm not afraid of her anymore. It's just like my musing says: <u>When you face your fears, they no longer have power over you.</u> That's how I feel. Alexandra doesn't have power to make me feel bad about myself anymore, and that feels good.

I'd better get going. Running late, as always! Good thing I already got dressed.

———∞———

Zenda jumped to her feet, sprinted into her bedroom, and tucked her journal under the pillows on her bed. Then she quickly stopped in front of her mirror. She had chosen a sleeveless pink dress today that fell just above her ankles. Small pink shrub roses—thorns removed, of course—formed the flower crown she wore around her head. The pale pink petals contrasted nicely with her bright blue eyes.

Zenda smiled and ran downstairs with Oscar following at her heels. Her parents, Verbena and Vetiver, sat at the breakfast table, sipping herbal tea and eating muffins. Zenda slipped into her seat, where her mother had placed a glass of peach juice and a bowl of dried fruit and crunchy grains drenched in fresh milk. Zenda picked up a spoon and began to eat.

Vetiver looked at Zenda's flower crown and smiled. "Lovely choice this morning, starshine," he said. "Are you still having problems with your crowns? I know your *kani* was giving you some trouble."

"It's getting better," Zenda said. "I think I can control it more."

That was true. *Kani*, the gift of communicating with plants, almost never materialized until a person turned thirteen. Even then, very few people on Azureblue had it. But Zenda had shown signs of *kani* early—something that made Verbena and Vetiver very proud, but that only made Zenda nervous. At first, she had no control over her *kani* at all, and her gift had caused her many embarrassing moments. Most involved her flower crowns, which tended to change their appearance to match her emotions.

Verbena reached over and stroked Zenda's hair. "I think you're doing a wonderful job, honey. You've been through so much these last few weeks. I hope you know your father and I are very proud of you."

Zenda's cheeks reddened. Her mom and dad could get so mushy sometimes.

"Thanks," she said, rising from her chair. "But I'm almost late, remember?"

Verbena stood up and kissed her forehead. "See you later, Zenda. Maybe we'll catch up with those spikeberries later."

Zenda sighed. "I knew it was too good to last."

Vetiver chuckled. "They're only spike-berries. You'll survive."

"Of course I will," Zenda teased back. "I survived Aquaria, didn't I?"

Her father stood up and gave her a hug. "Yes you did, starshine. Yes you did."

Zenda left the house and walked down the winding path that took her through the family's fields to the village road. Her parents owned Azureblue Karmaceuticals. They produced lotions, potions, and other products made from plants and distributed them all over the planet. They grew many of the herbs and flowers they used in their preparations.

A gentle breeze caused the wildflowers on the roadside to rustle as Zenda walked past. It was pleasantly warm, and the sun shone brightly in the blue sky overhead. Without realizing it, Zenda found herself humming a tune that her grandmother Delphina had taught her years ago.

This is going to be a good day, Zenda told herself. She had survived Aquaria, faced Alexandra, and earned more musings. Confidence boosted her step as she neared the Commons, a circle-shaped park in the center of the village.

All of the roads in the village led to the Commons, which was crowded with boys and girls on their way to school. Zenda scanned the crowd for Camille, her best friend, whom she usually met in the circle every school morning. But there was no sign of her.

Then Zenda saw a head of shaggy blond hair. She recognized Mykal easily, even without seeing his face. She and Mykal had been friends since they were little. After Mykal's parents had died in an accident last year, he began to spend more time at Azureblue Karmaceuticals, helping with the plants. Zenda saw Mykal almost every day lately, which was just fine with her. He seemed to take up most of her thoughts these days.

Zenda walked up to Mykal and tapped him on the shoulder.

"Ready to go back to school?" Zenda asked.

Mykal turned around and smiled. "Hey, Zen," he said.

Zenda noticed a girl sitting on a wooden bench in front of Mykal. She had light brown hair that fell in curls on her shoulders. Her green eyes were just a shade lighter than Mykal's. She smiled at Zenda.

"Are you Zenda?" she asked. "Mykal's been telling me about you. I'm Willow. I just moved here."

Of course, Zenda remembered. Her mother had told her that a new family had moved into the village. Zenda had forgotten all about it.

"That's me," Zenda replied.

Mykal began to talk quickly. "It's Willow's first day of school. She's from the village of Mara, near the Pearl Seas," he said. "Isn't that amazing? She's been telling me about all of the saltwater plants there. I've never even heard of some of them!" His eyes shone the way they always did when he talked about plants.

"That's great," Zenda said. "Have you seen Camille anywhere?"

But Mykal had turned back to Willow. "I've heard there are more than four hundred varieties of seaweed in the Pearl Seas," he said. "Have you eaten any of them?"

Willow laughed. "Probably all of them. My mom loves to make seaweed soup. She says it's the elixir of life—whatever that's supposed to mean."

Mykal laughed, and Zenda suddenly felt left out. She didn't know anything about seaweed, and it didn't seem like it would matter anyway. Mykal wasn't even paying attention to her.

"Well, I guess I'll find Camille," Zenda interjected. "School will start soon."

"You're right! I'd better walk you!" Mykal said.

Zenda felt better until she realized Mykal was talking to Willow, not her.

"You shouldn't be alone on your first day," Mykal was saying. "Besides, I'd like to find out more about the seaweed. It's hard to get it fresh around here."

Willow stood up and smiled at Mykal. "I am a little nervous about starting school," she admitted. "And I don't mind talking about seaweed." Then she looked at Zenda quizzically.

"How unusual," she said. "Are those green roses? I've never seen green roses before."

Zenda grimaced and took off her flower crown. The flowers had changed from pink to green.

"Looks like your flowers changed color again," Mykal said.

"That happens sometimes," Zenda muttered. "I'd better go."

Zenda walked away. Why had her flowers turned green? Before, blue flowers had turned red when she was embarrassed. Closed buds had bloomed instantly when she was impatient. So why had the pink flowers turned green?

At that moment, Camille walked up to her.

"What's wrong?" her friend asked, her dark brown eyes filled with concern.

"My flower crown started out pink, then it turned green," Zenda explained. "But I can't figure out why."

"What's that saying? 'Green with envy,'" Camille said. Then she shook her head. "No, that doesn't make sense. What would you have to get jealous about?"

Zenda blushed. "Nothing," she said quickly. She couldn't be jealous of Willow, could she? What was there to be jealous of? Just because Mykal suddenly had a fascination with seaweed?

"I guess it's just a fluke," Zenda said. "Come on. We'd better get to school!"

Koah

"Imagine that your legs are roots extending deep in the earth. Take a deep breath and visualize your roots sinking into the ground . . ."

At the Cobalt School for Girls, every morning began the same way: with Marion Rose, the girls' teacher, leading students in a grounding exercise to prepare for the day ahead. Normally, Zenda kept her eyes closed for the process, but today she had one eye open.

The girls sat on soft straw mats scattered around the middle of the room. Camille, as always, sat on Zenda's right. Her friend wore a crown of purple phlox in her hair and a white dress embroidered with tiny violets all over. Black, curly hair cascaded down her back, and her skin was the shade of a ripe hazelnut.

Sophia sat next to Camille. Just like every other day, she wore a pair of paint-splattered overalls. Her curly brown hair was pinned up in two ponytails, and her skin was tanned from hours of fishing in Crystal Creek with her brothers.

Alexandra White and her two best friends, Gena and Astrid, sat on the opposite end of the room. Alexandra's long, chestnut hair looked shiny and perfect, as always. But Zenda wasn't concerned with Alexandra this morning.

Her gaze traveled to her teacher, Marion Rose. Right next to her sat Willow, a perfect picture of concentration. She wore a linen top the color of wheat and a long, green skirt. She sat with her back straight and her hands folded on her lap, absolutely still. Zenda couldn't participate in the grounding exercise for more than thirty seconds without fidgeting.

Marion Rose opened her eyes. "Very nice this morning, girls. I think we could all use some grounding after our big trip," she said, and there were murmurs of agreement. Some girls began to stand up, but the teacher held up her hand. "Before we go to our learning stations, I have something special to tell you."

The teacher reached behind her mat and held up a wide, glass jar. Zenda could see something green inside the jar. Was it an unusual plant? She couldn't see.

"This is a caterpillar," Marion Rose explained. "In about two weeks, it will morph into an impossus butterfly."

There was a gasp among the girls. Zenda and Camille exchanged surprised glances.

The impossus butterfly had gotten its name because it was one of the most beautiful creatures on Azureblue. Its wings looked like they had been formed by tiny, shimmering rainbows. The colors shifted and changed depending on the butterfly's mood—or that was the theory, anyway.

Camille eagerly raised her hand. "Will we get to see it emerge from its cocoon?" she asked.

Marion Rose smiled at Camille's excitement. "Even better," she said. "Tomorrow, each of you will receive an impossus caterpillar of your very own. It will be your job to take care of the caterpillar until it transforms."

Zenda felt a little nervous jump in her stomach. She was comfortable around plants, even though her *kani* sometimes made things go wrong. But except for Oscar, she had never taken care of any animals—especially creepy-crawly ones. How on Azureblue was she supposed to take care of a caterpillar?

The girls began to talk in excited whispers. Marion Rose raised her voice. "The impossus butterfly is a beautiful creature, but remember that taking care of any living creature is a serious task. I will be counting on all of you to treat your caterpillars with love and respect."

Camille squeezed Zenda's arm. "I can't wait!" she whispered.

Zenda knew how happy her friend

must be. Camille loved insects as much as Mykal loved plants. She wanted to be an ethno-entomologist when she got older — a scientist who communicates with insects.

The thought made Zenda relax. Camille would help her. And how hard could taking care of a caterpillar be, anyway?

Marion Rose continued. "I'm also pleased to see that our new student, Willow, should have some valuable insight for us on this project." The teacher turned to her. "Willow, you couldn't have joined us at a better time. Why don't you tell us a little about yourself?"

Willow nodded. "I moved here with my mom, my dad, and my older sister from the village of Mara. That's by the Pearl Seas."

Knew that already, Zenda thought crankily.

"I started my gazing ball training in Mara," Willow continued. "I've received eight musings so far. I hope I'm not too far behind you all."

"Eight musings is wonderful," Marion Rose said.

Suddenly, Zenda's seven musings didn't seem like such an achievement.

"Willow also has a special gift that will help us with our impossus caterpillars," Marion Rose continued. She turned to Willow. "Is it all right if I tell them?"

Willow nodded.

"Willow has the gift of *koah*," the teacher said. "As you know, that is the gift of communicating with animals."

Willow's freckled cheeks turned pink. "It might be *koah*, but we're not sure yet. I can reach some animals but not others. And it doesn't always work."

"Hey, that's just like Zenda, only she's got *kani*!" Sophia announced.

Marion Rose nodded. "Yes, it's unusual to have two early bloomers in one class," she said. "We're very fortunate."

The teacher stood up. "Now that we

all know Willow, let's return to our learning stations. I've left some information about the impossus butterfly for each of you. Please read it all before you get your caterpillar tomorrow."

Zenda got to her feet and picked up her mat. Some of the girls gathered around Willow and began to ask her questions.

"What animals have you talked to?"

"Can you tell me what my dog is thinking?"

"How old were you when you got it?"

A bad mood settled over Zenda as she headed to her station. The fact that she had developed *kani* early had always made her feel awkward. But in a way, it had made her feel special too. She didn't feel so special anymore.

One by one, the girls headed to the learning stations. Most of their schooling took place in the Sage Building, a wide, U-shaped structure. Long, L-shaped desks crowded the room, one for each student. Each desk was as different as the girl who used it. Some were covered with rocks and stones; others sprouted all kinds of plants; art supplies were scattered all over Sophia's space. Zenda's was stacked with books, papers, and maps and drawings of the solar system. At the beginning of the year, each girl had picked a topic of independent study, and Zenda had chosen astronomy.

Today, a small book with a green cover sat on top of her copy of *Thirteen Planets*. She opened the book to a beautiful color picture of the impossus butterfly.

Zenda stared at it, lost in the rainbow pattern of its wings. She had seen one once, while searching for mushrooms with her father deep in the Western Woods. It had seemed unreal, almost, like a creature from another world or a fairy tale. The beautiful butterfly had danced through her dreams ever since.

Suddenly, the project didn't seem so bad at all. Zenda actually felt excited about it. She turned her chair around to face Camille's learning station, which was right next to hers.

"Isn't this going to be great?" Zenda began, but Camille wasn't there. Zenda looked around the room and saw Camille at Willow's desk. They were both bent over the picture of the butterfly. Camille was talking quickly.

"I'm hoping I'll get the gift of *enti* when I'm thirteen," she was saying. "I would love to be able to communicate with insects. But I heard that *koah* works with insects too."

Willow nodded. "It's mostly for mammals and birds, but it sometimes works with insects," she said. "A few weeks ago, I talked to a mosquito that tried to sting me."

"Really?" Camille's eyes were shining. "What was it like?"

Zenda suddenly felt angry. It wasn't even lunch yet, and already her two best friends had latched onto Willow like they had known her forever.

It's like she's put a spell on them, Zenda

thought, but as soon as it popped into her mind, she felt silly. Of course Camille would be interested in Willow's *koah*. All Camille dreamed about was being able to talk with creepy-crawly things. Willow's gift must be fascinating to her.

Zenda turned back to her desk and spent the morning reading through the book. It was filled with all kinds of facts and figures—the proper diet of the caterpillar, the ideal temperature for the cocoon stage. By the time Marion Rose announced lunch, Zenda's head felt like it was spinning.

Camille walked over to Zenda's station. "I can't wait until tomorrow," she said.

"Me either," Zenda said, and she meant it. "I'm a little nervous, though. It looks like taking care of the caterpillar isn't so easy. Maybe we could—"

At that moment, Willow walked up. "Can I have lunch with you two?" she asked.

Camille suddenly looked uncomfortable.

"Sure," she said. "I mean, you can have lunch with me. Zenda . . . I mean, Zenda doesn't . . ."

Alexandra White's voice interrupted her.

"Zenda goes home at lunchtime," she said with malice. "She broke her gazing ball."

Zenda turned around and smiled at Alexandra. "That's right," she said evenly. "I broke my gazing ball, so I don't go to gazing ball class."

"Uh, sorry," Willow said. "I didn't know."

"It doesn't bother me," Zenda said abruptly. She picked up the book. "See you later, Camille."

Zenda walked out of the classroom without looking behind her. She felt good about the way she had handled Alexandra.

But Willow . . . Zenda frowned. Willow seemed nice enough, but Zenda just didn't like her. She wasn't exactly sure why. And she definitely didn't like the idea of Camille eating lunch with her, when Zenda had to go home by herself. The green roses popped back into her mind.

"I'm not jealous of anyone," Zenda muttered firmly as she headed home.

Roots

"How's it going, starshine?"

Zenda looked up from her bucket of spikeberries to see her father standing on the other side of the berry patch. He wore his gray hair in a neat ponytail, as always, and his hazel eyes smiled at her through his wire-rimmed glasses.

Zenda looked down at her dress, which was now streaked with purple juice from the spikeberries. Tiny scratches covered her hands, caused by the sharp, prickly hairs that grew on the skin of the berries.

"It's going good," Zenda said. "If you like being drenched in sticky berry juice."

Vetiver smiled and sat down next to her. "It's a difficult prize, the spikeberry, but well worth it. Just one drop of spikeberry juice can cure twelve diseases that we know of."

Zenda sighed. Her father was always lecturing her on the powers of plants. She knew he was right, but it didn't make picking spikeberries any easier.

Vetiver read her expression. "Cheer up, starshine," he said. "I've come to tell you to take a break. You've been out here almost two hours."

Two hours? The time had passed more quickly than Zenda had realized. "Thanks!" she said brightly. "Is it all right if I go see Persuaja?"

Persuaja, a mysterious woman with the gift of psychic powers, had once helped Zenda after she had stolen a rare and dangerous orchid from her parents' greenhouse. The two had stayed close, and Zenda hadn't seen her friend in more than a week.

"I don't see why not," Vetiver answered. "Unless, of course, you have schoolwork to do."

Zenda thought about the impossus butterfly. She'd already read through the book—the real work would start tomorrow, when she got her caterpillar.

"Nothing today," she said.

Vetiver rose and picked up the bucket of

29

spikeberries. "I'll take these back. Have a nice visit with Persuaja."

Zenda quickly ran to the stream that passed through her family's fields and washed her hands. The cool water soothed her scratches. Then she returned to the path that led to the Commons.

Zenda had only known Persuaja for a short time—right after she broke her gazing ball. But already she knew the way to Persuaja's cottage by heart. Once she reached the Circle, she chose one of the paths that radiated from it like spokes on a wheel.

The path led to the Western Woods, a large expanse of tall trees on the edge of Zenda's village. She wasn't exactly sure how large the woods were; she did know that she had never gone into the woods and emerged on the other side.

Many people in the village traveled into the woods to meditate, search for herbs and mushrooms, or simply to walk and enjoy the sturdy beauty of the trees. But only one person lived there, as far as Zenda knew.

Nearly everyone on Azureblue discovered that they had some kind of special ability after they turned thirteen. Some, like Zenda, had *kani*—although Zenda secretly hoped she might discover another ability on her birthday. Others had gifts of healing, art, teaching, or other useful areas.

Only a handful had the gift of psychic ability, and Persuaja was one of them. People from all over the village traveled to her cottage deep in the woods, nestled inside a grove of hawthorns, for her advice and counsel.

Zenda reached the Hawthorn Grove quickly. The low, bushy trees protected Persuaja's cottage with their thorny branches. Zenda walked around the circle until she came to the entry, an archway created by carefully parted hawthorn branches. She stepped inside the grove.

There was Persuaja's cottage, a small

building made of gray stone and topped by a thatched straw roof. Herbs and flowers flourished in beds all around the cottage, something Zenda had always thought to be curious. There wasn't much sunlight in the grove, certainly not enough to grow herbs, but Persuaja's plants were as healthy and green as any in Zenda's family's fields. Zenda stopped to admire a patch of tall purple coneflowers, reaching out to touch one of the blooms.

A strange shiver came over her body, along with a feeling. Zenda paused and tried to isolate it. Sometimes her *kani* allowed her to pick up the emotions of plants. Zenda closed her eyes and kept her hand on the coneflower petals.

Worry. The feeling struck her clearly. But what could coneflowers possibly have to be worried about? Zenda silently delivered the question to the plants but didn't get a response. Just more worried feelings.

Zenda frowned and knocked on the door of the cottage. A large eye had been carved into the dark wood, and it seemed to stare at Zenda as she waited for the door to open.

"Come in!" Persuaja called from inside, and Zenda pushed open the door.

A fire burned in the fireplace on the southern wall, and Persuaja stood over it, stirring something in a large iron pot. The psychic wore a long robe made of soft, deep purple fabric. Her long, black hair had been swept up into a large pile on top of her head. Two ebony sticks seemed to be holding the whole mass of hair in place. Persuaja's myriad of bracelets jingled as she stirred the pot. She looked up as Zenda entered.

"So you've been picking spikeberries, have you?" Persuaja greeted her.

"Did you see a vision in the fire?" Zenda asked, impressed. Persuaja must have used her psychic powers to know that.

Persuaja's dark eyes twinkled. "No. I

saw the purple juice stains on your dress and the scratches on your hands," she said. "Sometimes good observation does the job just as well as a psychic vision."

Zenda laughed, then suddenly remembered the coneflowers outside. "This might sound strange, but when I touched the coneflowers on the way in, they felt worried," she said. "Does that make any sense?"

A look of concern briefly flickered across the psychic's face, then disappeared. "They are probably wondering when the next rains will come," she replied. "We haven't had a good rain in weeks."

Persuaja took a metal spoon from the pot and rested it against the hearth. She motioned to the overstuffed purple couch in the center of the room.

"Come sit with me, Zenda," she said. "A lot has happened to you since we last talked."

"You must have heard about Aquaria," Zenda guessed.

34

Persuaja nodded. "But I have not heard the story from you."

Zenda launched into the tale, ending with the story of how the seventh missing piece of her gazing ball had appeared.

"The musing says: 'A chance not taken is an opportunity missed,'" Zenda said. "I like that one. I was afraid to go to Aquaria, but I'm glad I went. Even if we did get lost."

Persuaja nodded. "You gained a great deal of confidence from that journey," she said. Then she frowned. "But I sense that something is causing your confidence to waver."

Zenda nodded, glad she had made the trip to Persuaja's cottage. The feelings she was having about Willow and the caterpillar project were hard to put into words, but somehow she knew Persuaja would understand.

"There's a new girl in school, Willow," Zenda said. "She's nice, but . . . everybody likes her so much. Especially Mykal and

35

Camille. She knows about seaweed, and she can communicate with animals."

"Willow is Willow, and Zenda is Zenda," Persuaja said. "You both have gifts to share. There is room in this village for both of you."

Zenda nodded. "I know. I don't want to dislike her. But I do, and I'm not sure why. Maybe it's because she just moved here, and she fits in with everybody so easily. I still don't feel like I fit in."

"Many children who move often learn to make friends easily, because they have to," Persuaja said. Her eyes drifted toward the fire, and Zenda realized that her friend looked tired and paler than usual. "I have lived on seven different planets, in countless villages. Moving to a new place is not always easy."

Zenda realized with surprise that she had never known where Persuaja had come from. She'd just assumed the psychic had always lived deep in the woods. "Why did you move around so much?" she asked.

"I do not know my parents," Persuaja said matter-of-factly. "As a baby, I was left on the planet Citrine in a village green. When I was old enough, I traveled from planet to planet, trying to find my roots. I never found them."

"I'm sorry," Zenda said. She couldn't imagine life without Verbena and Vetiver.

"I am not," Persuaja said. "I have met many wonderful people in my travels and learned many things. But remember that, for Willow, this part of her journey may not be so easy."

Zenda nodded. What Persuaja had said made perfect sense.

"And now I must get back to my potion," Persuaja said. "It does no good to over-boil crimson leaf."

Persuaja rose to her feet—and then, suddenly, her eyes closed. Zenda watched, helpless, as Persuaja sank to the cottage floor.

"Persuaja!" Zenda cried.

Sensitivity

Zenda ran to Persuaja's side and knelt down. Her friend was breathing, but her eyes were closed.

"Persuaja." Zenda shook her gently, but the psychic did not respond.

Zenda's heart pounded in her chest. The healers—she had to get Persuaja to the healers. But unlike most households in the village, Persuaja's did not have a horse or wagon, and Zenda couldn't lift her onto one, anyway.

Zenda hated to leave Persuaja alone, but there wasn't anything else she could do.

"I'll be back as quickly as I can," she said, hoping Persuaja could hear her.

Then she ran.

As she tore through the trees, Zenda tried to think. There were a few houses near the border of the woods. She'd have to try one of those.

Then Zenda remembered. The Baltis, a family of weavers, lived just off the eastern path. Camille's mother bought cloth there for her dressmaking. Zenda had visited there before. She found the fork leading to the eastern path, and a few minutes later came upon a large log cabin. A woman stood outside, tossing grains at a bunch of chickens.

"I need help," Zenda said. "It's Persuaja, in the woods. She's ill."

The woman must have noticed the look of panic in Zenda's eyes. She ran into the house without a word and came back with two men: a broad man with white hair and a beard, and a young man in his twenties with blond hair and sparkling blue eyes.

"Always worried about her out there by herself," said the older man. "I've got a stretcher in the barn. We'll get her and bring her back to the wagon."

Zenda followed the men through the woods to Persuaja's cottage. She watched anxiously as they gently lifted Persuaja onto the stretcher, which was a strong piece of canvas wrapped around a wooden pole on each end.

"Is she all right?" Zenda asked.

"She's hanging in," said the old man.

"The healers will help her," the young man said in a kind voice. "Don't worry."

The men jogged back over the trail with Persuaja in the stretcher. Zenda followed them back to their home, where the woman had hitched a gray horse to an open wooden wagon. The men slid the stretcher onto the wagon floor.

"You can ride back here with me," the young man said. Zenda gratefully climbed up into the wagon and held Persuaja's right hand. It felt cold.

"Giddyap!" the older man called, flexing the horse's reins, and the wagon lurched forward.

"I'm Lon Balti," the young man said. "That's my father, Diego."

Lon's voice was calm and soothing. Zenda smiled faintly.

"I'm Zenda," she said. "Thanks for

helping Persuaja."

"I'm sure she'll be fine," Lon said. "Thanks to your quick thinking. Was Persuaja telling you your future?"

"No," Zenda said. "We're friends." She looked at Persuaja's still face, and a wave of worry swept over her again.

Lon put his hand on Zenda's shoulder. "We're almost at the healing center."

The wagon pulled up to a low, white building a few seconds later. Diego and Lon carried the stretcher inside. Zenda followed them into a small room with walls painted a calm, peaceful blue. An indoor fountain bubbled soothingly in the corner.

A healer, a man in a blue robe, nodded as soon as he saw Persuaja. He opened a door for Diego and Lon to walk through. Zenda tried to follow them again, but the healer stopped her.

"Wait here," he said.

So Zenda sat on a couch and waited.

And waited . . . and waited . . .

"Wake up, Zenda."

Zenda sleepily opened her eyes. Her mother sat next to her, stroking her hair.

"Mom?" Zenda asked. When had her mother arrived?

"The healers sent a message to the house," Verbena answered. "I came as quickly as I could."

Then Zenda thought of Persuaja, and all of her sleepiness left her. "Is Persuaja all right?"

"The healers said you may see her now," Verbena answered.

Zenda nodded and rose to her feet. Another healer, a woman with red hair, walked through a doorway next to the fountain and beckoned Zenda to follow.

The healer led Zenda to another small room. This room was also painted blue, and the sound of soft chimes filled the air as they dangled in the open window. Persuaja sat in a bed, propped up on comfortable-looking blue and lilac pillows. She looked tired, but fine.

"You are up late, Zenda," Persuaja said.

"I'm worried about you," Zenda said. "Just like the coneflowers."

Persuaja nodded. "Perhaps I should have told you before, but I didn't want to worry you unnecessarily," she said. "I am ill, Zenda, and have been for some time now. The healers are doing everything they can to help me."

"But what's wrong?" Zenda asked. The healers on Azureblue were so skilled in their knowledge of plants that there was almost no sickness they couldn't cure.

Persuaja knew her thoughts. "The healers have not seen an illness like mine before. It is possible that my condition is unique to one of the other planets in our solar system. The task before us is to find out which planet that may be."

Zenda remembered their earlier conversation. Persuaja had no idea who her parents were, or where they were from.

Persuaja reached out and took Zenda's hand in hers. "Thank you for helping me, Zenda. But now you must go. I need my rest, and so do you."

"I'll come visit you tomorrow," Zenda promised.

Zenda and Verbena carried freshly picked moonglow flowers as they followed the path back home. The flowers cast a soft light so they could find their way. They walked in silence for a while.

"What's going to happen to Persuaja?" Zenda asked.

Verbena didn't answer right away. Finally, she said softly, "I am sure the healers will be able to help her."

Her mother's words made Zenda strangely uneasy, as though she were leaving something out. But Verbena didn't add anything else, and Zenda was too tired to ask anything further.

Zenda fell into a deep sleep as soon as she climbed into bed, but she woke up early the next morning, feeling anxious and awake. She pulled her journal out from underneath her pillow and began to write.

Last night was so scary. I am so glad we got Persuaja to the healing center in time. It looked like she might never open her eyes again.

Why can't the healers help her? There must be some plant on Azureblue that can cure Persuaja. I think V & V know something, but they won't tell me. Why do they treat me like a child sometimes? Persuaja is my friend. If something is really wrong with her, I deserve to know.

Maybe I can use my kani to help

47

somehow, although I don't know what I would even do . . . I feel so helpless! I just hope Persuaja's going to be okay.

Zenda was still thinking about Persuaja when she reached the Commons Circle later that morning. She didn't even notice Camille, Mykal, and Willow walking toward her.

"Hey, Zen!" Mykal called out, waving. "What are we, invisible?"

"Oh, sorry," Zenda said. "I've just been thinking about something that happened last night. I—"

"Can you believe we're going to get our caterpillars today?" Camille interrupted. It wasn't at all like Camille to interrupt, but Zenda could see how excited she was.

"I forgot," Zenda said, realizing she had forgotten. Right now, she had other things on her mind.

"Willow showed us her sketches of an impossus butterfly that she made on a hike once," Mykal said. "You should see her house. There are pictures of animals all over the place. Willow's really good."

"You went to her house?" Zenda asked sharply.

"Willow invited us yesterday, after school," Camille said. "We stopped by to get you, but Vetiver said you weren't home. Where did you go?"

Zenda suddenly didn't feel like talking about what had happened. If they had really wanted to know where she was, they could have asked Vetiver, she told herself. "I didn't do anything special," she said.

Mykal waved good-bye as he turned down the path that led to the Cobalt School for Boys. Zenda followed Camille and Willow to the girls' school.

Camille had worn a light-blue dress embroidered with butterflies in honor of the first day of the caterpillar project. Camille's mother made beautiful clothes that she sold in a dress shop in the village, and Camille always had something special to wear. Willow wore a light-green top with draping sleeves shaped like flower petals. Her dark green pants looked comfortable and baggy, but neat.

Zenda looked down at the dress she had picked out and frowned. She had been so worried about Persuaja all morning that she hadn't concentrated too much on her outfit. She hadn't noticed the wrinkles in her deep red dress until she had walked out the door, and her hastily made flower crown consisted of bright yellow buttercups that clashed with the color of the dress.

When they entered the Sage Building, they found the girls gathered around Marion Rose's desk. Glass jars covered the surface, and in each jar squirmed an impossus caterpillar. Marion Rose walked up to the desk, clapping her hands.

"Grounding first, please," she said. "Impossus caterpillars are very sensitive to human emotion."

Zenda wasn't the only one fidgeting during the grounding exercise that morning. Everyone seemed anxious to get their caterpillar. When they were finished grounding, Marion Rose sent everyone to their learning stations and called the girls up to her desk one at a time.

When Zenda's name was called, she approached the desk with a mix of excitement and nervousness. Marion Rose smiled and handed Zenda a glass jar.

"There are enough dogwood leaves in there to last until this afternoon," the teacher explained. "You'll need to make sure your caterpillar gets enough food and water over the next seven days. All the information you need is in your book."

Zenda nodded and took the jar back to her station. She carefully placed the jar down and looked through the glass. She hadn't gotten a close look at the caterpillar yesterday. Up close, it looked like many other caterpillars Zenda had seen in the fields. Its body was about as long as her index finger and covered with what looked like soft, green fur.

Curious, Zenda reached out to touch the fur but stopped herself. She should check the book first. Zenda flipped through the pages until she came to a chapter titled "Handling an Impossus Caterpillar."

Impossus caterpillars are tolerant of human contact, and some, in fact, seem to thrive on it. They are, however, sensitive to human emotions, so make sure you are well-grounded before proceeding.

To handle the caterpillar, extend your wrist in front of it. The caterpillar will sense your pulse and climb onto the wrist in response. From this position, it is possible to stroke the caterpillar's fur. You may hear a soft humming sound in response.

Zenda gently lowered her hand into the jar, palm up. Just as the instructions stated, the caterpillar crawled right onto her wrist, tickling her skin a bit. Holding her breath, Zenda lifted her hand out of the jar and rested it on her lap.

"Hey there, little guy," Zenda whispered. She slowly stroked its back. "I'll take good care of you."

Zenda waited to hear the humming sound. Instead, she noticed that the caterpillar began to change color! The pale green fur slowly transformed into a bright red.

Before she could react, she heard Marion Rose's voice over her shoulder. "Oh, dear! Didn't you read the section on color sensitivity?"

Zenda shook her head. "No," she said meekly. Had she done something terribly wrong?

Marion Rose smiled. "Thankfully, it's not serious. In fact, it's a great learning opportunity." She raised her voice. "Gather round, girls!"

The other girls approached Zenda's learning station.

"Can anyone tell me why Zenda's caterpillar has turned red?" she asked.

"That's easy," Alexandra offered without even raising her hand. "Because she held it near her red dress. Impossus caterpillars are sensitive to bright colors."

"Exactly," Marion Rose said. "The color change can cause harm to the caterpillar if it remains in this state too long. Can anyone tell me how we could help it?"

Alexandra had no response. The only girl to raise her hand was Willow. She stepped up next to Zenda.

"Like this," Willow said. She held out her wrist next to Zenda's caterpillar and let it climb on. Then she held it up to her pale green shirt. Immediately, the caterpillar began to change back to its original color.

"Excellent!" Marion Rose said, beaming. "I knew it would be wonderful having you in our class, Willow."

"Yes, we need someone to fix Zenda's mistakes," Alexandra muttered, just loud enough for Zenda to hear. Next to her, Gena and Astrid giggled.

Marion Rose clapped her hands. "Back to your stations, please. I hope we all learned something just now."

Willow held out her wrist next to Zenda's, and the caterpillar crawled onto Zenda's wrist.

"It should be fine," Willow said. "It wasn't red for very long."

"Thanks," Zenda muttered, and felt the red begin to fade from her own cheeks. She turned her back to Willow and let the caterpillar crawl off her wrist and back into the jar.

"Sorry," Zenda whispered to the caterpillar, and she felt her eyes fill with tears.

Her worst fear had come true. She knew taking care of the caterpillar couldn't be easy, and she had messed up after only a few minutes. The thought that she could cause the caterpillar to get hurt—or worse—made her feel terrible.

Then another thought struck her—how was she going to help Persuaja if she couldn't even take care of a caterpillar?

Lani

Zenda spent the rest of the morning reading through the book again, underlining anything she thought looked important. She wasn't going to take any more chances. She imagined her caterpillar transforming into the most beautiful impossus butterfly in the whole class—so beautiful that everyone would forget about what had happened that morning.

Right before lunch break, Marion Rose clapped her hands again. "In all the excitement about our caterpillars, I almost forgot," she said. "The Cobalt School for Boys has invited us to their school for a dance this weekend. It's a yearly tradition. I would have made the announcement sooner, but we forgot all about it when planning for the trip to Aquaria. I hope everyone can make it."

The room erupted into conversation as the girls shared their excitement about the dance. Camille rushed to Zenda's learning station.

"The dance sounds fun, doesn't it?" she gushed. Then her expression changed.

"I mean, I think it does. What if nobody dances with us? What if I start to dance, and everyone laughs? What if I don't wear the right thing? What if—"

"We go to dances in the village all the time," Zenda reminded her. "We always have fun. And no one ever laughs at you when you dance. You're a good dancer. Besides, your mom will make you something beautiful to wear."

Camille smiled. "Thanks, Zen. You always make me feel better."

Zenda glanced at her caterpillar and frowned. "I couldn't make my own caterpillar feel better. Willow had to do that."

"It was an easy mistake," Camille said. "And your caterpillar's fine, right? Aren't they cute?"

Zenda nodded and found herself smiling along with her friend. Camille always made *her* feel better too. "Mine's adorable," Zenda said. "It's so soft!"

"I can't believe we get to take them home," Camille said.

"Right," Zenda agreed. She'd have to take hers home early.

Sophia and Willow walked up behind Camille. "Ready for lunch?" Sophia asked.

Camille nodded. "We've got to talk about the dance. What color do you think I should wear?"

The girls began to talk about the dance, and Zenda sank into a bad mood again. Things had started to feel like normal again, talking with Camille just like old times — and then suddenly she felt left-out once more. She carefully gathered her caterpillar and book and left the Sage Building without saying good-bye.

Zenda arrived back home just as Vetiver was plopping down a huge salad and a platter of lightly fried nutcakes on the large kitchen table. Some of the karmacy staff were seated around the table. They often ate lunch together.

Zenda's mother was pouring glasses of cold blackberry tea out of a pitcher. When she saw Zenda, she smiled. Then she raised an eyebrow.

"Is that an impossus caterpillar?" she asked.

Zenda nodded. "It's for school. I have to take care of it until it transforms into a butterfly." She put the jar in front of her place at the table and sat down.

Vetiver wrinkled his nose. "Must we look at that creature while we're eating?" he asked.

"I have to keep it with me wherever I go," Zenda explained. "It says so in the book."

Verbena laughed. "I never understood your fear of bugs," she told Vetiver. "After all, your plants wouldn't be able to grow without them."

"I know," Vetiver said, sighing. "All right. The little guy can stay. Does it have a name?"

Zenda hadn't even thought of naming her caterpillar, but it sounded like a good idea. "Not yet," she said, searching her mind. Then she thought of Lon Balti, who had been so kind and helpful the day before. Maybe she could use his name somehow . . .

"How about Lani?" she suggested. She held her face up to the jar. "How do you like it?" The little caterpillar was busy munching on a dogwood leaf.

"I'd say that's a yes," said Vetiver.

Zenda's mood improved as she ate her nutcakes, which were crispy and delicious, and her salad. As she ate the green leaves, she wondered what it might be like to be Lani, eating leaves all day, getting ready for his big transformation. Zenda thought of her own quest to get the missing pieces of her gazing ball. Who would have thought she'd have something in common with a little caterpillar?

After eating, she helped Verbena and Vetiver do the lunch dishes.

"Starshine, think I can get another bucket of spikeberries this afternoon?" Vetiver asked as Zenda dried the last dish.

"Again?" Zenda asked. She held out her hands. "I'm still scratched from yesterday."

"You could wear gloves, of course," Verbena suggested.

"I hate gloves," Zenda mumbled. Gloves made her feel so awkward. She liked the feel of warm, brown earth and slippery, green leaves when she worked with plants. Picking the berries went much easier and faster with bare hands—even if the bushes were a little thorny.

"Just one bucket," Vetiver said.

"I'll do it," Zenda said. "Can I go visit Persuaja when I'm done?"

Verbena nodded. "Of course, honey."

A thought occurred to Zenda. She had hoped to find a way to help Persuaja. And here she lived in a house with the two most prominent makers of healing potions on the planet. Maybe her parents could help.

"Isn't there some way we can help Persuaja?" Zenda blurted out. "You both know so much about healing plants. There must be something we make here that can help her."

Vetiver looked solemn. "We make healing potions, Zenda, but we're not healers. If the healers need something from us, they will come to us, as they always do."

Tears stung Zenda's eyes. "But can't we at least try? The healers haven't found anything to help her yet."

Verbena knelt down and hugged her daughter. "I know you want to help, Zenda. But there's nothing any of us can do right now. I think going to visit Persuaja today will help her a lot. She loves to see you."

Zenda nodded, but she didn't feel much better. The whole situation made her feel helpless and frustrated.

"I understand," she said. Then she picked up the glass jar off the table. "Come on,

Lani. Let's go pick some spikeberries."

Zenda walked through the door and grabbed a bucket from the front porch. Then she headed to the spikeberry patch.

At the patch, Zenda set Lani's jar next to one of the bushes and knelt down beside it. She began picking the fat, purple berries.

"I'll get you some spikeberry leaves, too, Lani," she told the caterpillar. "The book said that impossus caterpillars like to eat spikeberry leaves."

As soon as she said the words, the spikeberry bush she was touching began to quiver. Soon all of the bushes in the patch were quivering.

"What's wrong?" Zenda asked. Then the answer suddenly came to her. She had mentioned the caterpillar, and the bushes had probably sensed it. They were afraid. It made sense. Just a few hungry impossus caterpillars could mean death to a spikeberry bush. She hadn't thought that

Lani's presence might bother the plants.

Zenda put both of her hands on the bush. *Don't be afraid*, she told the bushes. *I won't let the caterpillar eat you. I'm keeping him safe in a jar. I'll feed him something else!*

But the quaking did not stop. Zenda closed her eyes and concentrated again. Once the first bush calmed down, Zenda walked from bush to bush, sending the same message.

Finally, all of the bushes had calmed down. Zenda opened her eyes. Then she walked back to Lani's jar and picked it up.

"Sorry, Lani," she said. "I'll get you something else to eat besides spikeberry leaves."

Then Zenda gasped. The jar was still crowded with dogwood leaves—but nothing else. Lani had escaped!

Searching

"Lani! Lani!"

Zenda crawled through the spikeberry patch on her hands and knees. She had been searching for the caterpillar for almost an hour now, but it was nowhere in sight.

Zenda leaned back in the grass and stared up at the sky. A bird flew overhead, and Zenda got a hollow feeling in the pit of her stomach. In the book, she had read that impossus caterpillars were easy prey for all kinds of birds. Would Lani end up as someone's dinner?

Tears welled up in Zenda's eyes. This was all because of her *kani*. She had stirred up the emotions of the spikeberry bushes, and Lani had probably sensed that and crawled away. He could be anywhere.

Think, Zenda, she told herself. *There has to be some way to find Lani.*

Then she remembered being lost on Aquaria. She had never thought she would survive, but she, Mykal, Camille, and yes, even Alexandra, had worked together to find their way back to camp. She didn't have to do this alone. She could ask for help.

Zenda jumped up and ran through the village to Camille's house. Camille's father, Galen, pushed Camille's little sister, Lorelle, on a swing hanging from a tall oak tree in the front yard.

"Hello, Zenda," Galen said, smiling. "Been doing some work in the gardens today?"

Zenda looked down at her red dress, which was now streaked with dirt as a result of her search for Lani.

"Something like that," Zenda replied. "Is Camille here?"

"She left for Aponi's dress shop a few minutes ago."

"Thanks!" Zenda said, waving. "Bye-bye, Lorelle."

The little girl shyly waved back, then let out a happy cry as the swing rose higher in the air.

Aponi's dress shop wasn't far. Camille's family lived around the corner from the village shops. Zenda walked past a bakery, an aromatherapy shop, and a shop selling wooden rocking chairs before reaching the bright orange storefront of Magical Threads.

Zenda pushed open the door and stepped inside. The smell of sandalwood incense permeated the shop, flooding Zenda with an immediate feeling of peace and calm. Colorful dresses hung on racks arranged around the shop. Camille's mother, Aponi, stood behind a counter covered with sparkly beads. Aponi looked like a taller version of her daughter, with the same brown eyes and curly, dark hair.

"Zenda, how nice to see you," she said warmly. "Have you come to find a dress for the dance too?"

At that moment, Zenda heard a giggling sound to her right. She turned and saw Camille and Willow behind one of the dress racks. Camille held a purple dress in front of Willow.

"Hi, Zenda," Willow said. "What do you think of this one? Camille says purple is your favorite color."

"It's nice," Zenda muttered, suddenly feeling shy and left-out again.

Camille seemed to sense Zenda's feelings. "Mom's shop is on the way to Willow's house. I said I'd help her find a dress for the dance." Then Camille noticed Zenda's dress. "Is everything okay?"

Just tell her, a voice inside Zenda said. *Camille can help*. But something—she knew it was irrational—held her back. Part of her didn't want Willow to know she had lost her caterpillar. And another part of her thought, *Camille would rather spend time with Willow. She doesn't want to help you.*

"Everything's fine," Zenda said. "Have fun."

"Zenda, don't leave!" Camille pleaded.

"Something's wrong. I can tell. You've got to—"

Zenda didn't let her finish. She quickly turned and left the store.

By the time Zenda got home, Vetiver had supper on the table. Zenda ate her stir-fried vegetables in silence, watching the sun set through the large kitchen windows. Lani was out there somewhere, alone and helpless. Her eyes started to well with tears once again.

"Starshine, what's wrong?" Vetiver asked.

"Nothing," Zenda said. "May I be excused, please?"

"Of course," Vetiver replied. "Just let us know if you feel like talking."

Zenda walked upstairs and flopped on her bed. Oscar jumped up next to her and began licking her face. Zenda gently brushed him aside.

"Go away, Oscar," Zenda said. "Stay away from me. I can't take care of anything."

Oscar made a small whimpering sound. He walked away from Zenda, but came back a second later with a cloth doll in his mouth. He dropped the doll in front of Zenda's face.

Luna smiled at Zenda with her stitched-on grin. Zenda reached out and touched the doll's hair, made of colorful silk scraps. Luna had belonged to Zenda's grandmother Delphina when she was a little girl, and before she died, Delphina had passed Luna on to Zenda. Zenda often felt like the spirit of her grandmother lived on in the doll, somehow.

Zenda stared into Luna's green eyes, and a vision of her grandmother's face appeared in her mind's eye. In the next instant, a memory replayed in Zenda's mind.

When Zenda was eight, she and Delphina had baked a cake together. The cake layers came out lopsided, and the frosting was too thin. The finished cake looked like a mess. But Delphina was not worried.

She took Zenda out to the garden,

where they picked handfuls of edible pansies. Delphina washed and dried them and they arranged them all over the cake. The final result was beautiful.

"I may not be a good cook, but I am an artist," Delphina had said. "It's good to use the strengths you have to help you solve problems. You can do that, too, Zenda. Know your strengths."

The memory faded, and Zenda closed her eyes, deep in thought. *Know your strengths.* What had Delphina been trying to tell her?

Kani. Zenda knew that was one of her greatest strengths right now. But how could *kani* help her find Lani? She could communicate with plants, not with animals.

Then it dawned on her. She could ask the plants. The plants in the field could tell her where Lani went! Zenda sprang out of bed.

Zenda plucked a moonglow flower and headed back to the spikeberry bushes. The phosphorescent flower lit the way as she walked through the fields. When she reached the patch, she put her hand on one of the bushes and brought an image of the caterpillar into her mind.

The bush began to quiver. Zenda quickly addressed it. *Where did Lani go? Is he near here?*

The bush quivered some more, but then an image suddenly popped into Zenda's mind: the daisy field.

"Thank you," Zenda whispered. She ran to the field of daisies. Their white petals seemed to glow in the darkness. Zenda knelt down and touched one of the larger flowers. Once again, she conjured up a picture of Lani in her mind.

The daisy flower slowly bent to the right. Zenda walked over a few plants and touched one of the flowers there. She closed her eyes and thought of Lani.

This time, the plant bent backward slightly. Zenda walked a few plants back. She touched another daisy flower and focused on the little caterpillar.

Please, she thought. *If you have seen this caterpillar, please let me know.*

In response, the flower began to quiver with excitement. Zenda knelt down and held the moonglow flower near the daisy stem.

There, curled underneath a green leaf, was the tiny green caterpillar. Relief flooded over Zenda, and she held out her wrist next to Lani. He crawled over from the daisy stem, and Zenda lifted him close to her face.

"Don't worry, Lani," she said softly. "I won't let anything else happen to you."

Worries

When Zenda woke up the next morning, she immediately checked on Lani. The little caterpillar was safe in his glass jar, munching on dogwood leaves.

"Good morning, Lani," Zenda said. "I was so worried about you yesterday!"

As soon as the word "worried" left her lips, Zenda suddenly thought about Persuaja. She had forgotten to visit Persuaja in the healing center yesterday!

Zenda quickly threw on a yellow dress, grabbed Lani, and ran downstairs. If she left early, she could stop in the healing center on the way to school.

A healer in a blue robe greeted her when she walked in. "Your friend told me you might be coming this morning," said the healer, a small man with close-cropped brown hair. "She will be happy to see you."

Zenda followed the healer to Persuaja's room. The psychic sat in a rocking chair next to the window. She turned her head when Zenda came in.

"Good morning, Zenda," Persuaja said, giving her a soft smile.

"I'm so sorry I didn't come yesterday!" Zenda blurted out. "Lani—my caterpillar—got lost in the fields, and I spent the whole afternoon looking for him."

Persuaja motioned to a chair in the corner. "Tell me about it."

Zenda told Persuaja everything, including her encounter with Camille and Willow, and the vision of Delphina that she had seen. Persuaja closed her eyes and nodded as Zenda told her the story.

"Your grandmother was right," Persuaja said when Zenda had finished. "You were wise to use your strengths to find Lani. But it worries me that you did not turn to Camille and Willow for help. You are surrounded by people who love you, Zenda. There is no reason to face your troubles alone."

"I know," Zenda replied. "I can't explain

it. I just didn't feel like telling anybody about it."

Persuaja looked Zenda directly in the eyes, and Zenda could once again see the unusual tiredness there.

"Let me tell you a story," Persuaja began. "When I was twelve, I lived in a children's home on the planet Citrine. You may know that on Citrine, there is no gazing ball training before a child turns thirteen."

Zenda leaned forward, fascinated. Persuaja had never talked much about her life to Zenda before. In many ways, Persuaja was a stranger to her.

"Without gazing ball training, it can be difficult to handle one's gift when it manifests. When my psychic ability arrived on my thirteenth birthday, I wasn't prepared at all," Persuaja continued. "There was an older girl at the home, Mariah. She had psychic ability also, but she had spent two years in training. She could have helped me, but I was too proud to ask her. I didn't really like her, you see. She got a lot of attention."

Zenda immediately thought of Willow. "What happened?"

Persuaja smiled slightly. "Because I could not control my powers, I kept causing strange things to happen. Once I accidentally transported the whole home to a swamp."

Zenda laughed. "Did you really? That sounds like something I would do."

Persuaja nodded. "Finally, I asked Mariah for help. It wasn't easy for me, but she ended up being a great friend in the end."

Zenda could not imagine being friends with Willow. Still, she understood what Persuaja was trying to say.

"We all need help at one time or another," Persuaja continued, and the tone of her voice filled Zenda with worry again.

"How are you feeling?" Zenda asked.

"You will be late for school," Persuaja said, avoiding her question. "Thank you for coming to visit me. Perhaps you can check on my herbs for me sometime, Zenda. They will wonder what has happened to me."

"Of course," Zenda said. "I'll go as soon as I can."

An uneasy feeling traveled with Zenda as she walked from the healing center to school. She thought of Persuaja all during the grounding exercise.

At least I don't have to worry about Lani anymore, Zenda thought with relief.

Zenda spent the morning working on a written report about the solar system. She looked over the names of the planets—Crystallin, Stellata, Ouvaroff, Citrine—and thought of Persuaja. One of those planets was her home. But which one?

She was lost in thought when Marion Rose tapped her on the shoulder.

"Zenda, when was the last time your caterpillar ate something?"

"This morning," Zenda said, puzzled. "Why?"

"I've been walking around the room all morning, and I haven't noticed it eat once."

Zenda looked into Lani's jar. The caterpillar sat on the bottom of the glass, not moving.

"Has anything unusual happened since you brought it home last night?" Marion Rose asked.

Zenda hesitated. She wasn't about to admit to losing Lani—not in front of the class. Especially after what happened yesterday.

"No," Zenda lied.

Willow walked up to Zenda's learning station. "Maybe I can help," she suggested. "I tried communicating with Surya, I mean, my caterpillar yesterday, and I think I got some messages from it. Maybe your caterpillar could tell us what's wrong."

"I'm sure there's nothing wrong," Zenda said quickly. "Maybe he's been eating when we weren't looking. He was fine this morning. I'll keep an eye on him. I promise."

83

Marion Rose frowned. "I suppose. But if it doesn't eat anything soon, let me know."

Willow looked sad as she walked back to her station, and Zenda felt a pang of guilt. There was no harm in letting Willow help her. But what if Willow found out that Lani had escaped last night?

I'm sure Lani's fine, Zenda told herself. *If anything goes wrong, I'll tell Marion Rose.*

Zenda did not take her eyes off Lani all morning, even during botany class with Dr. Ledger. The caterpillar did eat a few leaves, but not anywhere near the amount he had eaten the day before.

Still, he ate something, Zenda told herself. *He's probably fine.*

Zenda decided not to worry Marion Rose. After lunch, she went right upstairs and started reading the impossus butterfly guidebook.

There was a whole chapter on eating habits.

An impossus caterpillar, on average, must eat five pounds of green leaves a day in order to survive. If your caterpillar has stopped eating or is not eating enough, there could be several causes.

First, check the mineral content of its water. Well water may contain some minerals harmful to impossus caterpillars. Use spring water instead.

Next, make sure your caterpillar is not exposed to too much sunlight. In nature, the caterpillars spend daylight hours in the shade.

Correcting these factors should restore your caterpillar to its regular eating habits. If not, seek help from a qualified entomologist. A caterpillar that does not eat the required amount of food every day will not live to cocoon stage.

The last sentence chilled Zenda. She couldn't let Lani die.

"But Lani will be fine," Zenda said out loud. The book seemed pretty straightforward.

She'd get Lani the freshest water from Crystal Creek. And she'd move him from her desktop to a secluded spot on her bookshelf.

By the time Zenda went to sleep, she had given Lani fresh water and dogwood leaves. The caterpillar munched on a leaf as Zenda placed him on the shelf.

Zenda watched Lani eat as she wrote in her journal.

Everything is going wrong!

I am so worried about Persuaja. She doesn't seem like herself. She cuts me off when I ask her about herself. She may want to spare me from worrying about her, but I can sense that something is wrong. Really wrong. I just wish she would tell me! And I've been so worried about Lani, too, that I haven't even thought about how to help Persuaja.

I know Persuaja said I should let people help me with my problems. And I will. But I think Lani is going to be fine. The book said so, right?

Tomorrow night is the dance. Everyone at school is excited about it, but I haven't even thought about it. Maybe it will be fun. Mykal will be there . . . I wonder if he will dance with me?

I will try to think positively, like Vetiver always says. Tomorrow, Lani will be eating, Persuaja will be better, and Mykal will ask me to dance.

I can dream, can't I?

———————

The Dance

Zenda checked on Lani first thing the next morning. The caterpillar had eaten some of the dogwood leaves, but not many. Zenda frowned.

Persuaja was right. She would have to ask for help, even if it meant admitting that she had let Lani escape. There was no school today, but Zenda knew Marion Rose would not mind a visit.

She headed to Marion Rose's cottage after breakfast. The teacher lived on the edge of the Western Woods. Everyone in the village knew where Marion Rose lived, thanks to the large, painted wooden sculptures on her lawn. The sculptures didn't look like people or animals, just interesting shapes that seemed to welcome visitors as they walked in.

Zenda rang the bell next to the red door, and Marion Rose answered, carrying a cup of tea in one hand. She wore her thick blonde hair in a long braid down her back; this morning, two paintbrushes were sticking out of it.

Marion Rose looked down at Lani's jar. "Is everything all right? Come in and tell me about it."

Zenda sat down at the kitchen table, which was covered with jars of paint in different colors.

"Lani is eating, but not a lot," Zenda said.

The teacher smiled. "That's a nice name," she said. "What kind of water are you giving it?"

Zenda explained that she had read the book carefully and followed the instructions, but Lani still wasn't better. Marion Rose frowned.

"I'm stumped, Zenda," she said. "I do this every year, and we've always been able to help caterpillars that aren't eating properly. Has anything happened that would make Lani sick?"

Zenda took a deep breath. "I had Lani out in the fields the other day, and he got out.

But I found him a little while later, and he seemed fine."

Marion Rose frowned. "You're lucky he didn't get eaten by a bird," she said, and Zenda blushed. "But I'm glad that you found him. And you are coming to me for help. It still doesn't explain why Lani isn't eating, though."

The teacher looked thoughtful. Then her face brightened. "Have you talked to Willow yet? Maybe she can help you figure out what's wrong."

"Not yet," Zenda admitted.

"Keep doing what you're doing," Marion Rose said. "Lani might just need a little time. I'll see what I can find out in the meantime."

Zenda thanked her teacher and headed out. On the way home, she stopped at Persuaja's cottage. She reached out to the purple coneflowers. An emotion immediately flooded over her.

Sad.

Persuaja is at the healing center, Zenda told the flowers. *They are helping her. She will be home soon.*

Zenda could feel the flowers relax a tiny bit. She sighed. There wasn't anything else she could do.

When she arrived home, she found Camille waiting for her on her front porch.

"Why did you run out of the store yesterday?" Camille asked. "Something's wrong, Zen. You've got to talk to me. I'm your best friend!"

Zenda looked at her friend's worried face. All this time, she had been worried about Lani and Persuaja, and Camille had been worried about her.

"You're right," Zenda said. "Let's go up to my room."

Zenda and Camille sank down on the silk floor pillows in Zenda's room.

"Things have been crazy," Zenda began.

"The other day, when you came to see me, I went to see Persuaja. She collapsed in her cabin, and the Baltis took her to the healing center."

"Oh, Zen, that's awful!" Camille said, her eyes wide. "Is she all right?"

Zenda shook her head. "I don't think so. They don't know what's wrong with her."

"The healers will figure it out," Camille said. Zenda wasn't so sure; everyone said that, but the healers hadn't done anything so far.

"There's more," Zenda said. "Lani is sick. I took him to the fields the other day and he escaped. I found him that night, but now he won't eat. I don't know what's wrong, and Marion Rose doesn't either."

Camille looked like she might cry. "Zen, this is terrible! Why didn't you tell me sooner?"

Zenda shrugged. "I thought you were busy with Willow," she said.

"You're my best friend," Camille

reminded her. "Willow's new, and she doesn't know anybody. And she's really nice. She could probably help you with Lani if you ask. You could talk to her tonight."

"Tonight?" Zenda asked.

"At the dance," Camille said.

The dance! Zenda had almost forgotten about it. She had been so worried about Lani and Persuaja.

Zenda collapsed back into her pillows. "Oh, no! I haven't even thought about it. And I don't have anything to wear."

"I'm sure we can find something," Camille said. She hopped up and gave Zenda her hand. "Let's look in your closet."

Zenda opened the closet door, and Camille began sorting through Zenda's dresses, talking quickly. "I talked to Mykal yesterday. He said he and Ferris and Torin and Darius will meet us in the Commons tonight at seven and walk down with us. Willow and Sophia are going to meet us there too."

Camille's excitement started to rub off on Zenda. She began picking up dresses and holding them up to the mirror in front of her.

"Ooh, how about this one?" Camille asked. She took out a long, white dress made of two layers of fabric: soft white underneath, and a pale, see-through green over it. "You could wear a crown of baby lilies."

"That would be nice," Zenda admitted, and suddenly felt filled with warmth. It seemed like ages since she and Camille had gotten together like this, just for fun. It felt like everything was back to normal.

Everything Camille had said made sense—even the part about asking Willow for help. Zenda felt silly for not doing it sooner.

"I'll talk to Willow tonight, if you think she'll help me," Zenda said.

"I know she will," Camille answered. She gave Zenda a hug. "I'd better go. I know it's early, but I want to get ready for the dance!"

It was just growing dark when Zenda approached the Commons Circle at seven o'clock. Verbena had offered to watch Lani for her, and sat through nearly a half hour of instructions and explanation that Zenda had given her. Zenda had put on the green and white dress and a crown of baby lilies, just as Camille had suggested.

Mykal and his friends were standing in the Commons, laughing and talking. Mykal wore a green shirt and pants, like he always did. Next to him were Torin, a short boy with a mop of brown hair; Ferris, a tall boy with pale skin and bright red hair; and Darius, a dark-haired boy with skin the color of an acorn. The boys all looked a little cleaner than usual, Zenda noticed.

"Hi, Zenda!" Mykal called out. "Ready to dance?"

"Sure," Zenda said, her face blushing slightly. Maybe Mykal would ask her to dance after all.

Sophia approached next. Zenda had never seen her in a dress before, but tonight she wore a red dress and a crown of red roses in her hair.

"Nice dress," Ferris teased. "You look like a tomato."

Sophia laughed and pointed to Ferris's shirt, which had been dyed with at least ten different swirly colors. "Nice shirt. Did a rainbow throw up on you?"

That cracked up all of the boys. Zenda admired how natural and easy Sophia seemed around everyone, especially boys. Zenda guessed it probably had to do with the fact that Sophia had four older brothers.

"Hey, look," Ferris said through his giggles. "Here comes a grape and a lemon."

Zenda turned to see Camille and Willow—Camille in a pale yellow dress with orange suns embroidered on it, and Willow in the purple dress from Aponi's shop.

"I think they look nice," Mykal said.

"Thank you," Willow said. "Camille's mom made this dress, so you can't say anything bad about it, Ferris."

"That's right!" Camille added.

Just then, the sound of drumbeats came from the distance.

"Enough talking," Ferris said. "My feet feel the beat!"

Ferris took off down the path that led to the boys' school, and the others followed him.

Zenda gasped as the school came into view. Like the Cobalt School for Girls, the Cobalt School for Boys was made up of four U-shaped buildings arranged to form a circle. A tall oak tree sat in the center of the circle. Tonight, lanterns containing fresh moonglow flowers hung from the branches, illuminating the circle. Musicians had set up around the foot of the tree: two women playing hand drums, a man playing bells and other percussion instruments, and another man and woman, each playing guitars. Some boys and girls were already dancing, while others stood on the sidelines, sipping lavender punch that was being served by Wei Lan, the headmaster of the boys' school.

Ferris turned to Sophia and bowed low. "Shall we dance?" he asked.

"Sure," Sophia replied, and they went and joined the dancers.

Darius was standing next to Camille. He looked down at his feet.

"Uh, I'll dance if you want to," he said.

"That would be nice," Camille said, smiling brightly.

Zenda's heart began to beat faster as Camille and Darius began to dance. Mykal was tapping his foot and moving his body to the beat. Surely he'd want to join his friends.

"Want to dance?" Mykal asked.

Zenda was about to respond when she realized that Mykal was looking at Willow, not her. Willow smiled shyly. "That would be great."

Zenda felt like she had been stung by a bee. Mykal had asked Willow to dance! He obviously liked Willow better. Even though he had only known Willow for a few days. It just wasn't fair.

To add to her misery, she saw Alexandra grinning at her from a few feet away.

"Poor Zenda," Alexandra said. "Nobody will dance with you, will they?"

"I don't see anyone dancing with you, either," Zenda shot back.

Alexandra scowled and walked away. Torin tapped Zenda on the shoulder.

"Will you dance with me?" he asked, a hopeful smile on his face.

Zenda suddenly felt miserable, as though nothing would cheer her up. "Thanks, Torin," she said. "I just don't feel like dancing tonight. I'm really sorry."

Then she turned and headed up the path.

The Key

Zenda got as far as the Commons Circle and stopped. She sat down on a bench.

She knew she was being silly. There was no reason to leave the dance. She could be dancing with Torin, having fun.

It was like her feelings had control over her, she mused. And she was feeling so many feelings at once. Worry about Persuaja and Lani. Confusion about Mykal. Jealousy toward Willow.

Yes, jealousy. She had known that all along. But she couldn't help it. Seeing Mykal ask Willow to dance had hurt.

But it was no reason to leave. She was always running away from things. It was time to go back.

As Zenda stood up, she saw Mykal coming toward her.

"Zenda, what happened?" he asked.

"I just needed some fresh air," she said. "It's okay. I'm coming back."

"Camille said you've been worried about

things lately," Mykal said. "Is everything all right?"

Mykal's green eyes looked so kind, and Zenda wondered how she could ever have been upset with him. "Persuaja's sick, and they don't know what's wrong with her," she said. "And there's something wrong with my caterpillar too. Marion Rose doesn't even know what to do."

"You should ask Willow to help," Mykal said.

Zenda cringed slightly. She was tired of hearing it—but she knew Mykal was right.

"I will," Zenda said. "Let's walk back."

"Willow's really nice," Mykal said as they walked. "It hasn't been easy for her. She only lived in Mara village for a little while. She's moved around a lot. Aunt Tess says it's important to make people like that feel at home wherever they go."

Zenda felt a pang as she thought of Persuaja traveling around the universe, looking to find her home. She suddenly realized how Willow must feel.

Mykal and Camille had seen it right away, and they had been nice to Willow, because that's how they were. The best friends anyone could want.

They neared the school, and Zenda stopped. "To tell you the truth, I was jealous of Willow," she said. "I felt like you and Camille were ignoring me. I don't know why I acted that way. It doesn't feel good at all."

Suddenly, the sound of tiny bells filled the air. A small light sparked in front of Zenda, and a piece of glittering crystal appeared out of nowhere. Zenda smiled and held out her hand.

The crystal shard—a piece of her broken gazing ball—dropped into her palm. Green mist swirled on the surface of the shard, then formed into words:

Jealousy is the lock that closes your mind and heart; understanding is the key that opens them.

Mykal looked at Zenda and grinned. "Would you like to dance?"

Zenda tucked the gazing ball piece into the silk pouch she wore around her neck. Then she held out her hand.

"Absolutely!"

Reaching Out

Before the night was over, Zenda danced with Mykal, Ferris, Torin, and Darius until her feet felt like they couldn't dance another step. As the dance wound down, the friends gathered under a maple tree drinking lavender punch.

"This is so much fun," Willow said. "I was supposed to go to a dance in my last village, but we moved right before it."

"Maybe you'll get to stay here until the next dance," Camille said hopefully.

Willow smiled. "That would be nice."

Zenda took a deep breath. "Willow, could I talk to you for a minute?"

"Sure," Willow said. The two girls stood up and walked to the edge of the school grounds.

"I just want to say that I'm sorry if I've been unfriendly to you," Zenda began. "You've been really nice to me. I hope I didn't hurt your feelings."

"It's okay," Willow said sincerely.

110

"Camille told me you're worried about your friend and your caterpillar."

"That's what I wanted to ask you," Zenda said. "I'd love it if you would come take a look at Lani for me. If you still want to help me, I mean."

"Of course," Willow said. "I know how I feel about Surya. I'd hate it if anything happened to him."

The two girls smiled at each other, and Zenda wondered how she could ever have had bad feelings about Willow.

"Want to get some more punch?" Willow asked. Zenda nodded.

The party ended soon after, and Zenda was so tired when she got home that she threw her dress over the top of her armchair. But she was awake enough to write in her journal.

I got my eighth musing tonight! It came after I finally admitted I was

111

jealous of Willow, and how wrong I was to feel that way. I apologized to Willow, and Mykal asked me to dance. All in all, it was a pretty great day. It also felt really good to talk to my friends about what's bothering me. It makes it easier to deal with somehow.

Lani still isn't eating a lot. I'm glad Willow's coming over tomorrow morning. I hope we can save Lani! If anything happens to him, I'll feel terrible.

Willow showed up the next morning, right after breakfast. Zenda brought Lani down on the porch, and they sat in a shady spot.

"How does your *koah* work?" Zenda asked.

"It's hard to explain," Willow said. "I

usually have to touch the animal. Then sometimes it's like . . . a feeling washes over me. Or pictures, or even words sometimes."

"That's just what *kani* feels like!" Zenda cried. "Only with plants. It's pretty amazing, isn't it?"

"Yes, it is," Willow replied, and the girls exchanged knowing smiles. Then Willow's face grew serious. "All right. Let me try."

Willow lowered her hand into the jar, and Lani climbed on her wrist.

"It's harder with insects," Willow said. "*Koah* can work with insects, but it's not as easy as with other animals."

Zenda watched as Willow closed her eyes and began to breathe deeply. She remained like this for several minutes. Then, suddenly, she frowned.

"Did you get anything?" Zenda whispered.

"It's like . . . a tummy-ache," Willow said. "Not a hungry tummy, but like Lani ate something bad. Does that make sense?"

She opened her eyes.

"I've mostly been feeding him dogwood leaves," Zenda said, thinking. "Unless . . ."

"What?"

"I didn't tell you, but Lani escaped in the fields the other day," she said. "I found him with the daisies. Would daisies hurt him?"

Willow shook her head. "No, impossus caterpillars love daisies. But maybe he ate something else in the fields—something he shouldn't have."

"That could be it," Zenda agreed. "I think I know how we can find out."

Zenda led Willow to the spikeberry patch. "We started out here," she said, pointing. "And the daisy field is over that way."

The girls walked toward the daisy field. They passed a hedge of rosebushes.

"Rose leaves shouldn't have hurt him," Willow said, looking around. "Is there anything else growing between here and there?"

Zenda thought. "Just some wild ice

violets," she said, pointing to patches of tiny silver flowers growing along the pathway. "We had some shipped here from the north, and they started spreading out of their bed. Now they grow everywhere."

"I don't know anything about ice violets," Willow said.

"Did somebody say ice violets?"

Camille and Mykal appeared from behind the rosebushes.

"We think Lani ate some ice violets when he got loose the other night," Zenda explained. "But we're not sure if that would have made him sick."

Camille looked thoughtful. "Impossus caterpillars don't live in the north. Ice violets would not be something they'd normally eat in the wild. You're probably right that the ice violets are to blame."

Zenda frowned. "Then this has never happened to an impossus caterpillar before. How are we supposed to help him!"

"I have an idea," Mykal said. "Follow me to the main greenhouse."

Two large greenhouses with rounded roofs sprouted on the border of Azureblue Karmaceuticals. They contained growing plants and served as a research laboratory for Vetiver and Verbena, who formulated all of the karmacy's products.

Vetiver was grinding herbs with a mortar and pestle when they walked in. He waved hello without looking up. Mykal led them to a shelf of books and pulled out one titled *Wildflowers of the Northern Lands*.

The girls watched as he flipped through the pages. He stopped, read for a minute, and then smiled.

"I thought so," he said. "Ice violets contain a high amount of a compound called askar."

"But askar is poisonous to impossus caterpillars!" Camille cried.

"Exactly," Mykal said. "But there's an

antidote. Anything high in acid will neutralize the askar. Maybe that's what Lani needs."

"How about lemon leaf?" Zenda said. The herb got its name from the citrus-scented oil collected by breaking its leaves.

"That might work," Camille said. "Lemon leaf won't hurt Lani, anyway."

Zenda ran and retrieved some fresh lemon leaf from the gardens. She put a leaf in the jar.

"Come on, Lani," she coaxed. "Take a bite."

But Lani didn't move.

"Let me try," Willow said. She reached in the jar and stroked Lani's back. In a few seconds, Lani began eating the leaf.

"Wow!" Zenda said.

"Let's just hope it helps," Willow added.

But the lemon leaf seemed to have an immediate effect. Once he finished the lemon leaf, Lani began hungrily munching on the dogwood leaves around him.

"I think it's working," Zenda said. "Thanks so much, everybody. I should have asked for your help sooner."

Zenda had barely finished her sentence when another missing piece of her gazing ball appeared in the air, accompanied by the sound of tinkling bells. Zenda caught it in her palm and watched the sky-blue musing form on the surface of the crystal:

Sometimes it takes more courage to ask for help than to act alone.

"Now that's really something, starshine!"

Zenda looked up from the crystal to see her father standing nearby, a look of awe on his face.

"Good work, Zenda," he said.

Zenda looked at Mykal, Camille, and Willow and smiled.

"I can't take credit for this one," she said warmly. "We earned this musing together!"

Cocooning

Vetiver invited everyone to stay for lunch, and he whipped up a huge batch of sesame noodles that they washed down with cold lemonade, sitting on the porch. They spent the rest of the afternoon talking. Zenda kept Lani nearby, and happily watched as he ate leaf after leaf after leaf. It looked as though Lani was making up for lost time!

The next morning, Zenda woke up thinking of Persuaja. She had two new musings now that she wanted to tell her about. And of course she wanted to know if the healers had been able to help Persuaja. But that would have to wait until after school.

Zenda slipped on a dress the color of a tangerine. She brushed her long hair until it shone. Then she went to the bookcase to get Lani.

Zenda gasped. Lani was gone—but this time, he hadn't escaped. Instead, a pale green cocoon sat nestled in a dogwood branch.

Zenda held up the jar and turned it

around and around. The cocoon looked like a tiny gift, a perfect package with a present inside. In a few days, an impossus butterfly would emerge. Zenda couldn't believe it.

When she got to school, she found that almost all of the caterpillars had formed cocoons during the night. Marion Rose looked delighted.

"The cocoons will hatch in about four days," she told them. "Times will vary, so you may want to keep them near you so you won't miss it. It's quite a sight to see."

A short time later, Zenda was busy writing about the planet Ouvaroff when Marion Rose approached her.

"I'm glad to see that Lani made it to the cocoon stage," she said. "Did you ask Willow for help?"

Zenda nodded. "I'm glad I did. She figured out that he had eaten something wrong, and then Mykal and Camille helped us figure out how to make him better. I

121

couldn't have done it without them."

"Good for you, Zenda," Marion Rose said. "I like to see my students solving problems creatively. But I always knew you could."

"I didn't," Zenda admitted. "I was so nervous in the beginning. I didn't think I could take care of a caterpillar at all."

"But you did," Marion Rose pointed out.

"Yes, I did," Zenda realized. "And I guess I would do it again. Now that I've done it, it doesn't seem so scary anymore. Thank you for believing in me."

Zenda went to turn back to her report when, to her amazement, another piece of her gazing ball appeared. The room grew quiet as the girls watched the crystal shard fall into Zenda's hand.

You can turn your weaknesses into strengths.

The musing was etched on the crystal in deep purple. Camille rushed to Zenda's side.

"Zenda, it's raining musings for you lately!" her friend said. "How many does this make?"

"This is number ten," Zenda said. Ten musings! She only had three more to go before she had them all.

Willow walked up. "That is so amazing, Zenda," she said. "I know it must have hurt when you broke your gazing ball. But getting your musings like this is almost better, isn't it? It seems so exciting."

Zenda nodded. "I never thought of that before." Until now, she had thought that breaking her gazing ball was one of the worst things that had ever happened to her. And even though getting her pieces back hadn't been easy, it had definitely been interesting. Of course, she wasn't done yet.

Persuaja would be so happy. Zenda tucked the crystal shard into her pouch.

She couldn't wait until lunchtime.

When it came time to go, Zenda headed straight for the healing center. There was no one to greet her when she entered, so she walked right to Persuaja's room.

Three healers leaned over Persuaja's bed. Her friend lay back against the pillows, her eyes closed. Her face looked as pale as a moonglow flower.

One of the healers—the man she had seen earlier—saw Zenda standing by the door. He hurried to her side and guided her to the hallway.

"Is she all right?" Zenda asked.

"Your friend fell into a deep sleep early yesterday," the healer told her. "She has not yet awoken."

"What do you mean?" Zenda asked.

"As your friend told you, we are not sure what is wrong," he said. "Her condition has become quite serious. But don't worry. There is still hope."

The healer gently led Zenda to the front door. "Persuaja needs her rest," he said. "But I will send a message to your family when you may come visit again. We will do everything we can."

The healer squeezed Zenda's free hand, then rushed back down to Persuaja's room. Zenda stepped out into the sunlight and stood, unable to move.

The healer had said there was hope. But they hadn't been able to help her yet.

Zenda leaned against the building and cried.

Hope

Four days later, Zenda sat at the dinner table, picking at her sesame noodles.

"I'm sure the healers will send a message soon, Zenda," Vetiver said, knowing the source of her worry.

"It's been days," Zenda complained. "I'd like to at least see her."

"I'll tell you what," Verbena said. "I'll go down to the healing center in the morning and try to get some answers for you. Okay?"

Zenda nodded. After supper, she helped with the dishes in silence. Then she grabbed Lani's jar and headed out to the porch. She had become so used to carrying the jar around with her that she didn't even think about it anymore.

Zenda climbed up on the porch swing and curled her legs underneath her. Oscar padded out onto the porch and climbed up on the swing next to her, curling by her side. Zenda held the jar in one hand and petted Oscar with the other, staring up at the twilight sky.

The setting sun colored the sky with brilliant shades of red and orange, reminding Zenda of hibiscus flowers. A few stars became visible, twinkling against the deep crimson background.

Zenda stared at the stars and wondered, as she had so many times these last few days, where Persuaja's family was, where she was from. Surely the answer to helping Persuaja lay out there somewhere.

"I wish I could talk to you, Persuaja," Zenda whispered. "I wish I knew that everything was going to be all right."

From her side, Oscar began to whimper softly. Zenda looked down.

Lani's cocoon had begun to stir. Zenda lifted the jar closer to her face.

The sticky, green strands forming the cocoon were breaking open. Zenda watched as a butterfly with a pearlescent white body crawled out of the opening. Its closed leaves were white on the underside.

"Good morning, Lani," Zenda whispered.

The butterfly wiggled its antennae, the only part of its body that still had any fuzz left. Then it slowly opened its wings.

Zenda understood then and there how the butterfly had earned its name. It truly was impossibly beautiful. Rainbow colors swirled on its wings, seeming to move on their delicate surface.

The butterfly flew out of the jar and landed on Zenda's arm for a second. Then it waved its antennae once more, as though saying good-bye, and flew off toward the fields.

Zenda watched the butterfly go, a little sad. Marion Rose had told them that the butterflies would stay close to the place where they were hatched. Zenda hoped she would see it again.

But at least she had seen it.

Lani's cocoon opened today! It truly is one of the most beautiful things I have ever seen. I am so lucky that I got to see it emerge.

I wonder if this was some kind of sign from Persuaja? I'd like to think so. Persuaja and Lani became ill around the same time. I thought I'd never be able to help Lani, but Lani got well. If Lani could be cured, why not Persuaja?

I was thinking about her when Lani came out. It was almost like a miracle, watching the butterfly open its wings.

Maybe Persuaja will get a miracle too.

If I see Lani again I will give him a new name.

Hope.

So much is happening all at once! I can't believe I have ten musings. I still need three more, though, and my thirteenth birthday is coming up in a few weeks. I'm not sure what will happen if I don't have all of my musings. All of the other girls will complete their training and find out what special gifts they possess. What if I don't finish? Will I stay twelve-and-a-half forever?

I guess there is nothing to do but wait and see what happens!

Cosmically yours,
Zenda

zenda

Check out the Zenda website at
www.zendabooks.com